Withdrawn

THE
Awesome
Atlanta
MYSTERY

Editor: Janice Baker
Assistant Editor: Sherri Smith Brown
Cover Design: Vicki DeJoy
Content Design: Randolyn Friedlander

Gallopade International is introducing SAT words that kids need to know in each
new book that we publish. The SAT words are bold in the story. Look for each
word in the special SAT glossary. Happy Learning!!

Gallopade is proud to be a member and supporter of these educational organizations
and associations:

American Booksellers Association
American Library Association
International Reading Association
National Association for Gifted Children
The National School Supply and Equipment Association
The National Council for the Social Studies
Museum Store Association
Association of Partners for Public Lands
Association of Booksellers for Children
Association for the Study of African American Life and History
National Alliance of Black School Educators

This book is a complete work of fiction. All events are fictionalized, and although the names
of real people are used, their characterization in this book is fiction. All attractions, product
names, or other works mentioned in this book are trademarks of their respective owners and
the names and images used in this book are strictly for editorial purposes; no commercial
claims to their use is claimed by the author or publisher.

Once upon a time...

Hmm, kids keep asking me to write a mystery book. What shall I do?

Mimi

Write one about spiders!

Papa said …

Why don't you set the stories in real locations?

That's a great idea! And if I do that, I might as well choose real kids as characters in the stories! But which kids would I pick?

MiMi, PiCK ME, PiCK ME!

ME, TOO, MiMi, PiCK ME, TOO!

Christina

Grant

Pick me!

You two really are characters, that's all I've got to say!

Yes you are! And, of course I choose you! But what should I write about?

National Parks!

SCARY PLACES!

Famous Places!

FUN PLACES!

Disney World!

New York City!

Dracula's Castle

GRAND CANYON

On the *Mystery Girl* airplane ...

I Can FLY us anywhere!

Or aboard
the *Mimi!*

*Take me to the
Forbidden City!*

Or by surfboard,
rickshaw,
motorbike,
camel ...

All great ideas!
I can put a lot of history,

MYSTERY,

legend, lore, and **laughs** in
the books! We can use other boys and girls
in the books. It will be educational and fun!

*Good
stuff!*

And can you put some
cool stuff online?
Like a Book Club and
a Scavenger Hunt and
a Map so we can
track our adventures?

Can I
apply?

And so, Mimi, Papa, Christina, and Grant took off aboard the *Mystery Girl* and America's National Mystery Book Series—where the adventure is real and so are the characters! —was born.

START YOUR ADVENTURE TODAY!

1

GOLDEN DOMES AND SESAME PEOPLE

"It's making me dizzy up here!" moaned Grant. He plopped his monstrous hamburger oozing with ketchup and mustard onto his plate. His head dropped into his hands. His upper body swayed to and fro. "AUUURRRGGG!" he pretended to gag as Christmas music played in the background.

Grant, Christina, and Mimi were eating lunch at the Sun Dial Restaurant. The restaurant was situated at the top of the Westin Peachtree Plaza Hotel in downtown Atlanta. The hotel sat on the highest geographical spot in Atlanta. Its restaurant slowly rotated 360 degrees above the Atlanta skyline.

"Quit being so dramatic, Grant. We're not going that fast," said Christina, shaking her head at her brother. She placed a forkful of pecan-coated chicken in her mouth. "What's that over there, Mimi?" she asked her grandmother.

Mimi turned her head to the left. Her gold and red stone earrings dangled. "That is Turner Field, where the Atlanta Braves play baseball," she replied.

"It's 'The Ted'! 'The Ted'!" yelled Grant. He forgot about his dizziness and jumped up to swing an imaginary baseball bat for his favorite team.

The kids were having a "Stump Mimi" contest to see if she could name whatever they pointed to as they circled around the Atlanta landscape.

Mimi, a writer of children's mysteries, had grown up in Atlanta. They were visiting the capital of their home state of Georgia for several days while she researched a new book.

Christina leaned forward and pointed downward. "Is that a cemetery down there?" she asked.

"Yes, that's Oakland Cemetery," answered Mimi. "Margaret Mitchell, who wrote *Gone With the Wind*, is buried there. So is the famous golfer Bobby Jones and lots of Confederate soldiers. There are a lot of really old graves there, too. Some of the founders of Atlanta are buried there."

Grant looked puzzled. "The first people who settle an area are called founders," Christina said to him.

"Did they find this restaurant when they came?" asked Grant, looking even more perplexed.

"No," said Mimi. "Back then, this place was just a bunch of streams, hills, forests, and Indian trails. See where those five streets come together? That's called Five Points. And over there is the Georgia Tech campus."

"Those people look like a bunch of little sesame seeds on a bun," said Grant. "Look! Compare!" He held up a couple of sesame seeds from his own bun.

"I think you've got something there, Grant," said Mimi. She squinted her blue eyes to focus on Grant's sesame seeds.

"What's that big rock out there?" asked Grant. Tomato soup drooled from his mouth.

"That 'big rock' is Stone Mountain," said Mimi. She wiped her napkin across his chin before the soup could find a home on his blue shirt. "That is one of the biggest exposed pieces of granite in the world!"

"Did they dump it out of a cement truck?" asked Grant. He laughed at his own silly joke.

Mimi laughed, too. "No, but there's a carving as big as a football field on it of—"

"Howdy, partners!" A booming voice interrupted their conversation. Christina looked up to see her grandfather's long, lanky form headed their way.

"I don't think you can wear cowboy boots in this place," Grant said to his grandfather.

Papa swooped his black cowboy hat from his head and slid into the fourth chair at their table. "If I can't wear my boots, I don't go," he said, tousling Grant's unruly blond hair.

"How's the *Mystery Girl*?" asked Christina. The *Mystery Girl* was Papa's little red and white airplane.

"She's getting her annual physical," Papa said and chuckled. "Got to make sure she's ready to roll in case Mimi wants us to go flying off somewhere to research her books. Now, I'm ready to get a head start on my Christmas shopping," he added, winking at the kids. "It takes time to find Mimi a present she doesn't already have."

"Well, you have about four weeks to find the perfect gift," said Mimi. She tossed her short blond hair and gave Papa a sparkling smile. "The kids are going to meet up with Christina's friend Leah and Leah's cousin Philip Smith. They are going to get the fabulous, five-star, native's tour of Atlanta while I do my research."

"There's no one better to show them around," said Papa and smiled.

"Why are those little people climbing all over the top of that round thing over there?" asked Grant. Everyone looked in the direction of the Georgia state capitol, glittering like a jewel beyond and below them. Men on scaffolding were walking on top of the capitol's dome.

"Hmmm," said Mimi, raising her eyebrows. "I don't know."

Christina looked up the question on her smartphone. "According to the Atlanta newspaper, the *Atlanta Journal Constitution*, they are cleaning and repairing the gold leaf on the dome," she announced. "It's been exposed to the elements for years now and needs a makeover."

"That whole dome is covered with GOOOOLD?" asked Grant, his blue eyes growing wide.

"It is," said Mimi. "It's sheathed in gold panned from creek beds in the old gold mining town of Dahlonega, Georgia."

"We learned in Georgia history class that Georgia is a 'gold rush' state," said Christina. "People always think that the first gold rush was in California in 1849, but gold was found in the North Georgia mountains in 1828."

"Wow," said Grant. "If Georgia had all that gold, why didn't they build Disney World here?"

As they slowly revolved past the capitol, Christina peered at the gold dome and the men repairing it. "Look, you can tell where they've been working," she said. "It does look shinier on one side. I guess that's the part that's been cleaned already. The other part looks pretty dull."

"Looks like mustard to me," said Grant. He wiped a wad of bright yellow mustard off his nose and held it up for the others to see.

Everyone laughed. Christina's blue eyes lingered on the dome until it was out of sight. She thought about what it must be like to stand on top of the dome and lay gold taken straight out of the hills and streams of Georgia.

As Grant would say, "Wow!"

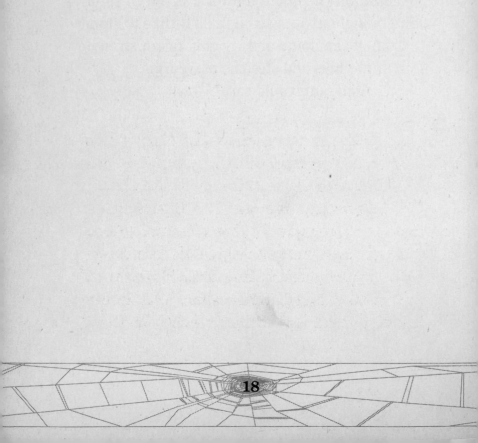

18

2
GOING DOWN?

Christina pushed the "down" button. She, Grant, Mimi, and Papa began their swift descent in the glass elevator that clung to the side of the Westin Peachtree Plaza Hotel.

"I think my hamburger wants back out," said Grant. Both arms were folded around his tummy, and he looked white.

"Hang in there, fella," said Papa gently. "Just a couple of floors on this one and then we'll be in the inside elevator. It's not so bad there."

Christina, who was better at heights than Grant, enjoyed the view of Atlanta. *Good idea*, she thought, noticing a man in a three-piece, pinstripe suit looking in the direction of the capitol through his binoculars. But he was leaning so hard against the glass that Christina thought it might break. Now, *her* stomach flip-flopped. *That's like the opening scene in a murder mystery*, she thought.

Once on the interior elevator, the ride was slower but a lot more crowded. She heard Grant moan beside her.

"Concentrate on something else," she said to him.

"I'm trying to," he whispered. "But I feel like I'm going to throw up on this man's shoes."

Christina realized the man next to Grant was the one who had been using the binoculars. He looked nervous. *Maybe he thinks Grant is going to throw up*, she thought. Grant took Christina's advice and concentrated on a red, white, and blue button on the man's lapel that read: BE AWARE, VOTE O'HARE.

Suddenly Grant slumped into the man.

"Sorry, sir," he mumbled. "I've had too much hamburger AND I don't like elevators."

After what seemed like eighteen light years, the elevator thudded to a stop. The man began barging his way out even before the doors opened. "Mister, you dropped—" Grant stuttered as he bent over to pick up a piece of paper from the elevator floor. But the man had vanished into the crowded hotel lobby. Grant stuck the paper in his jacket pocket.

Four spins through the revolving door later and Grant, Christina, Mimi, and Papa were out in the bright sunshine and crisp air.

"There they are!" Christina shouted. Leah and Philip were standing next to the doorman waving to them. Dark, curly hair framed Leah's face. Her brown eyes sparkled. Philip pulled a red sock hat over his short brown hair. He gave a cool "thumbs up" gesture to Grant.

"OK, kids, you all keep Mimi out of trouble," said Papa, waving goodbye to the group. "I'll see you this evening."

"You ready to head to Underground, Grant?" Mimi asked.

Grant nodded. He wasn't sure what "Underground" was, but Mimi sure seemed excited about it. "Mimi, if I can't see at Underground," said Grant, "will you buy me a flashlight? Or maybe one of those hats with a little light like miners wear?"

"If you can't see, I'll do it," said Mimi cheerily. "Follow me!"

Mimi, Christina, and Leah plowed through the crowd in the direction of Atlanta's Underground.

"Let's go, bro," said Philip. "Are you OK?"

"Yeah, I'm feeling better," said Grant, starting to walk. "I wish I could have given this note back to the man who dropped it, though." He fished for the paper in his jacket to show Philip.

From out of nowhere, a big, hairy hand appeared. "Gimme that note, kid!" a man snapped to Grant.

Surprised, Grant could only stare. Then, he stuck his scrawny arm further into his pocket and pulled out a piece of paper. "Sure, take it!" he said quickly.

The man grabbed the note and stuffed it into the pocket of his filthy jacket. He smiled a yucky, yellow-toothed smile. "Thanks, kid," he snarled and strutted off down the street.

"Should we scream?" asked Philip.

"I don't know," said Grant. "Either that or laugh—because why would anyone want my homework assignment? All I've got now is some note a man in our elevator dropped."

"Boy, I'd like to hear you give your teacher that excuse!" said Philip.

The boys giggled and scampered off to catch up with Mimi and the girls. They did not notice another man in a black trench coat standing in the shadows. He pulled his collar up and followed them down the busy street.

24

3

FORTUNETELLERS AND STRANGERS

"It's hard to keep up with your grandma," said Leah, as she and Christina power-walked behind Mimi.

"I know," said Christina, looking over her shoulder at Grant and Philip. "Come on, you guys!" she yelled.

Mimi crossed a street and then stopped next to a towering metal sculpture. The kids rushed up to her.

"OK, Christina and Grant," Mimi said. "Remember when I pointed out Five Points to you from the top of the Peachtree Plaza? Well, here it is! This is where five streets come together."

Mimi made five jabs at the knot of streets that joined there in a snarl of people and traffic.

"Before the white settlers came," she explained, "this was the intersection of two Creek Indian trails, the Pitch Tree Trail and the Sandtown Trail."

"What's a pitch tree?" asked Philip.

"It refers to a pine tree," replied Mimi. "Later, the white settlers probably turned the word into Peachtree. After the settlers came, a lot of these downtown streets were cow trails, leading from one settler's property to another's."

Grant looked nervously at the cars and trucks whizzing by in all directions. "I wouldn't want to be a cow trying to get home around here now!" he said.

"What's that metal sculpture?" asked Leah, looking up.

"That is the Five Points Monument," said Mimi. "It was built for the 1996 Atlanta Olympic Games to honor this historic intersection. See the trusses? Those represent the trolley tracks that used to cross here. The part that looks like a water tower actually represents a real artesian water tower that once stood here."

"You are a good tour guide, Ms. Marsh," said Leah, her brown eyes twinkling.

"Thank you, Leah," said Mimi, spinning around in her red high heels. "Now, we're going to walk down Peachtree Street to get to Underground. Be careful and keep up."

"I will!" Leah said, looking confused. "How does anyone find their way around here?"

"Just like everyone else finds their way around Atlanta," said Mimi. "Follow Peachtree and ask directions!"

As the group walked, Mimi told the story of Atlanta. First, the town was a little settlement called Thrashersville. It grew up around a store not far from where they were walking. Then the center of town moved to the Zero Mile Post.

"What's a zee-row-mile-post?" asked Grant.

"I know!" offered Christina. "The Zero Mile Post was where the railroad engineer of the Western and Atlantic Railroad drove a stake into the ground. The stake marked the end of the railroad line back in 1837."

"That's right," said Mimi. "He named the spot Terminus. As the town grew, it got renamed Marthasville, and finally Atlanta."

"Where is the Zero Mile Post?" asked Leah.

"It stood along the tracks for years," said Mimi. "But now, the Georgia Railroad Freight Depot encloses it. It's just a block away."

The kids followed Mimi down into what looked like a black hole. They left the sun and noise and crowds behind. They entered Underground—a city beneath a city. It was 20 degrees cooler and more than just a little spooky.

"Whooa! Where are we, Mimi?" asked Grant, shivering.

"This is Underground Atlanta!" Mimi replied. "Years ago, all of these streets were above ground. But there got to be so much train traffic that people and their horses and buggies couldn't get around very easily. So they started building bridges over the train tracks."

"Like bridges over the interstate highways?" asked Grant.

"That's right," said Mimi. "Before long, there were so many bridges over the tracks that they nearly covered up the old streets. People began to call this section of the old historic streets 'Underground.'"

"Now I get it!" said Grant. "It's UNDER GROUND! Like a cave!"

Mimi smiled and patted his head. "Look around, but stay together," she continued. "I have to talk to some people. I'll text you when I'm done."

The kids wandered into a brightly lit emporium filled with old-time musical instruments. A player piano and a miniature calliope tinkled and hooted simultaneously. Leah stuffed a nickel in a monkey's belly, and it added the tinny clang of its cymbals to the cacophony.

"Are you still feeling bad, Grant?" asked Christina. His face was white and he was acting weird. Before Grant could answer, she plunked a dime into a machine. A glass-encased dummy fortuneteller began to move spastically over a glowing crystal ball. Her ghostly mechanical voice grated, "YOUR FORTUNE IS ..." Then, she shuddered to a halt as the machine spit out a small piece of paper.

The kids gathered around as Christina read the fortune:

> A TALL, DARK STRANGER
> IS ABOUT TO ENTER YOUR
> LIFE. BEWARE OF HIM!

"Sure," Christina said. "And I'm going to find a pile of gold and fly without wings, too."

She stuck the fake fortune into her pocket and headed for the hot popcorn bubbling in the top of the silver cauldron of the perking machine in the corner. The kids each bought a small bag and wandered back outside.

After the circus atmosphere of the emporium, the streets of Underground seemed darker and more deserted than ever.

"It's hard to believe they left a neat place like this covered for more than 80 years before they turned it into shops and stores," Christina remarked.

The kids paused to look at some old brownish photographs in a window. They depicted the area in its heyday of horses and carriages. Men with pocket watches checked their train schedules. Women in long dresses carrying parasols tried to keep their petticoats from dragging in the red Georgia dust.

"Can't you imagine all the cobwebs that accumulated down here during that time?" said Leah.

"And the rats!" Grant added.

"Mimi says she used to come here when she was a girl before it was renovated," said Christina. "She's brought us here before."

"She has?" said Grant. "I don't remember."

"See, here is an old lamppost she showed us before," said Christina. "A shell from General Sherman's artillery hit it during the siege, right before the Battle of Atlanta began. Look, here's the mark—July 22, 1864. The sign says the shell ricocheted and exploded. It killed a freed slave named Solomon Luckie. He was a well-known barber in town. He was leaning against the pole talking to some other businessmen. Anyway, they carried him to a doctor's office to have his leg amputated, but he died a few hours later."

"That's terrible," said Philip. "An African American man was one of the first casualties of the Battle of Atlanta."

The kids were halfway down an especially narrow, dark alley when they stopped and looked at each other sheepishly.

"Why don't we check out something else that doesn't look so much like a dead end?" Christina suggested.

"Good idea," said Grant, still looking a little pale.

All of a sudden, the kids stopped dead in their tracks. Coming toward them was a tall, dark stranger in a black trench coat. Christina fingered the fortune in her pocket and cringed.

4
A CLOSE ENCOUNTER OF THE PRETZEL KIND

Christina grabbed Leah's arm and began backing up in the alley. "Let's get out of here," she whispered to the kids.

Suddenly, the figure in the trench coat broke into a big smile and stuck out his hand to Christina. "Hi," he said.

Instinctively, Christina extended her hand and shook his.

"Christina," said Grant, "you know we're not supposed to talk to strangers!"

"I know you kids don't know me," the man said hurriedly. "I just wanted to say you really shouldn't be down here alone. I was taking a shortcut to my car when I spied you four heading in this direction. I thought I should warn you."

To Christina's relief, he began to walk them back out of the alley. At the entrance to the street level, he mumbled something. Then he tipped his hat and disappeared into the shadows.

"Was he weird, or what?" Grant asked, hurrying up the steps.

"Maybe just a Good Samaritan," Christina replied. But she didn't feel positive about it. *I wonder why he used the words "spied" and "warn,"* she thought. *It sounded like he muttered, "Go find your grandma," before he vanished. How could he know about Mimi?*

As if by magic, Christina's phone beeped. The kids jumped. It was Mimi. Christina read her text message, "Meet me on street by pretzel vendor."

"WoooHoooo!! Let's go," said Grant. "I love pretzels!"

I guess I'm just too apt to see a spy behind every post, thought Christina. *But that's easy to do when the post is an old, candle-flickering streetlamp right out of a Sherlock Holmes story or a Stephen King novel. And the could-be-a-spy shows up in a black trench coat, no less!*

Grant charged up to Mimi with Philip on his heels. "Even if I bust wide open," Grant said, "I've got to have a hot pretzel!"

The kids sat on the curb next to one of Atlanta's little parks, while Mimi chatted with the pretzel vendor. Grant smeared his pretzel with brown mustard. Soon, the front of his shirt wore the same color. Digging into his pocket for a napkin, he plucked out something white, wadded it up, and wiped his mouth and shirt.

"You know, that's not a napkin," said Philip. "It's a piece of paper."

"Rumph grghn," Grant said, which is a mouth-full-of-pretzel mumble for, "Oh yeah, I forgot about that." With one hand, he unfolded the note and stared at it.

"What's that?" asked Christina.

"Just a note that man in the elevator dropped," Grant replied. "You know, the guy whose shoes I almost threw up on. It says something about 're-con-ver-shun.' What does that mean?"

Christina took the note and tried to make sense of it through the mustard stains.

Au Reconversion Process -

83984658903E

"Anything important?" asked Leah.

"Not really," said Christina. "Just some scrawled-out numbers about a reconversion process. It's not even **legible**."

She handed the note back to Grant. Grant wadded it up.

"Did I tell you about the guy who made me give him my homework?" asked Grant.

"What!? No, you didn't!" said Christina. "What happened?"

"This big, ol' hairy guy comes up to Grant and says, 'Give me that note!'" said Philip. "Grant swooped his homework out of his pocket. The creep grabbed it and went running down the street." The boys broke into gales of laughter.

"Wait until I tell Ms. Bingel that one!" Grant screeched. He and Philip slapped hands in a high-five, still giggling.

"Let's go to the Fox Theatre," called Mimi.

"Yeah, let's get out of here," said Christina. "All those buses lined up over there make me think a million people are going to charge out of these skyscrapers and trample kids like us."

Christina followed Mimi and the kids to a nearby MARTA bus. MARTA is the name of the public transportation system in Atlanta. She watched as Grant took the wadded-up note and tossed it into a trash can. A slight breeze caught the note, and it floated lazily into the can. "Gone with the wind!" Grant cried.

Suddenly, a man in a uniform sprang in front of Mimi. Christina saw him pound on the bus doors. He spoke briefly to the driver, who looked confused, then shrugged his shoulders tiredly. With a yawn and a stretch, the driver relinquished his seat and got off the bus.

"Howdy, ma'am," said the new bus driver jovially. "Watch your step! I'll take you wherever you want to go." He closed the bus doors behind Christina.

"The Fox Theatre," said Mimi with a smile.

But Christina wasn't smiling as she boarded the bus and took her seat with Leah behind Mimi. The driver looked creepy. He slowly pulled the lumbering bus out into Peachtree Street traffic.

5

BUS JACKED!

Grant and Philip settled down on the big, empty back seat of the bus.

"I need a nap," said Grant, yawning. "There's nobody on this bus except us." He put in an earbud, handed one to Philip, and cranked up the volume on his iPod.

Christina leaned her head against her window to watch the scenery. In tour guide mode, Mimi was turned around in her seat, telling Leah about the dozens of streets in Atlanta named Peachtree "something."

It was a grand afternoon. Everything the bus passed was bathed in a soft orange glow. Even though the city was beginning to bustle with people heading for the surrounding suburbs at the end of the workday, they seemed to move in slow motion. Mimi and the kids had ridden for a dozen blocks. The peach patches of sunlight on the sidewalks were fast turning lavender.

Suddenly, Christina felt something was wrong. *We're heading out of the city*, she thought, as the bus turned onto Ponce de Leon Avenue.

"Why didn't we stop at the Fox Theatre?" Christina called to the driver.

The bus bolted forward. Mimi's conversation stopped. Christina turned around and saw Grant jerk out his earbud. She noted the rows of empty seats. *Why haven't we stopped to pick up any other passengers?* she thought. Then she snapped forward toward the driver. He grinned maliciously at her in his rearview mirror.

"Driver!" Mimi called sharply, motioning to him. "You have missed our stop!"

Christina climbed over Leah and stood in the aisle. She grabbed a safety strap and tried to move forward up the aisle. Her body swayed violently as the bus continued to pick up speed and dodge cars.

"Hold on, Christina! I'm coming!" Grant screamed behind her.

Suddenly everything changed. With a sudden laser blast of blue light, a police car began to wail. The bus driver slammed on the brakes. Christina tumbled halfway down the aisle like a bowling ball. The driver dashed off the bus and down an alley.

Within seconds, a policeman hovered over Christina. "You OK, Miss?" he asked, helping her up.

"Sure," Christina said, but she was not sure.

"What's going on?" Mimi demanded, climbing out of her seat.

The policeman turned to Mimi and said, "We just got an anonymous tip that someone was trying to rip off a city bus. Didn't have anything to do with you. You just picked the wrong bus to ride this afternoon!"

"We certainly did!" said Mimi, straightening her scarlet jacket. She looked down the aisle of the bus. Her eyes flew wide open and her face paled.

Alarmed, Christina followed Mimi's gaze. A mussed Philip was standing near the open back door, crying. And Grant was gone!

6
MUSTARD AND MORE MUSTARD!

Four happy people tumbled out of the Atlanta police car. They threw their arms around a scruffy looking Grant, who stood in front of the Westin Peachtree Plaza.

"How did you get here?" asked Mimi, tears of joy streaming down her face.

"A policeman brought me," Grant said. "I fell out of the bus when that bus-jacker jerked open the doors."

"I'm going to find Papa," said Mimi. "This has been horrible. We need to turn this trip around. I'll be right back."

When Mimi disappeared into the hotel's revolving doors, Grant turned to Christina.

"I didn't tell Mimi everything," he admitted.

"What?" said Christina, jerking up her head.

"Remember the tall, dark guy in Underground? When I fell out of the back of the bus, he was there getting out of this neat, mustard-colored Mustang," Grant explained. "He helped me up. Then, he sent me over to a policeman who brought me back here."

"That's too much of a coincidence," said Christina. "It couldn't have been the same guy. Did he wear a trench coat? Did he say he had met you before?"

Just then, Mimi and Papa flew out the doors of the Peachtree Plaza.

"Is everyone OK?" Papa asked, visibly upset by their ordeal.

"We're OK," said Christina. "We just need hugs."

"Hugs it is!" said Papa. He wrapped his big arms around them all and squeezed tight. "I think we should have a fun night," he said. "Let's go to The Varsity for some chili dogs and cheese fries."

"After that," said Mimi, "we're going to the Fox Theatre to see the Atlanta Ballet perform *The Nutcracker*. We were headed there to pick up tickets for tonight when this whole fiasco occurred."

Christina and Leah clapped their hands. "Yeah! *The Nutcracker*!" said Christina.

"Awesome! The Varsity!" chimed in Grant.

Papa's car pulled up to the curb. He tipped the valet while everyone climbed in.

"Whew! I'm glad we're not taking the bus!" exclaimed Grant. "I don't think I can take another crazy bus ride!"

It was twilight. The city lights and traffic lights and street lights all twinkled red and green and white in the purple dark like a giant video game.

Now that it was over, everyone joined in telling and acting out parts of the afternoon's great bus ride adventure. But Christina pressed her nose against the cool glass of the window, watching for the mustard Mustang.

Then, Papa pulled into The Varsity, the world's largest drive-in restaurant. They cruised around three times to find a parking space. Music blasted over loudspeakers. People were everywhere. The smell was intoxicating.

"I love The Varsity," said Philip.

"ME TOO!" agreed Grant.

A number of chilidogs, onion rings, fried pies, and frosted oranges later, the kids belched their way out of The Varsity drive-in.

Grant whispered to Christina, "I think I spotted the Mustang just a second ago. I must have mustard on the brain."

"You sure got enough on your shirt," said Christina. But she, too, was on watch.

A few minutes later, they pulled up in front of the fabulous Fox Theatre. Everyone craned their necks to see the turrets.

"It's just like a palace," Mimi said.

"Is this where they had the premiere of *Gone With the Wind*?" Christina asked. Christina knew that the book's author, Margaret Mitchell, was an Atlantan. She had read parts of the book for a school report. The scenes describing the Civil War battles in and around Atlanta were bloodily realistic.

"No," she heard Mimi say. But Christina never heard the rest. Her mind and eyes were fixated on a corner where she could have sworn a mustard-colored Mustang had just breezed out of sight.

48

7
CLOAK & DAGGER, CLOAK & DAGGER

The inside of the Fox Theatre was right out of *The Arabian Nights*, a famous collection of Persian and Arabic folk tales. Spongy-thick oriental carpets...walls draped in thick tapestries...thick marble pillars...miles of red velvet rope and gold tassels. Christina half expected a mummy to take their tickets!

The kids loaded up with popcorn, mints, and gummies and found their seats. Mimi and Papa were just a couple rows in front of them. High above their heads hung an incredibly lifelike night sky, complete with twinkling stars and wispy clouds.

"WHOOOOOPS!" said Philip. "I just spilled my bag of popcorn."

"I really need to go to the restroom," said Grant.

Christina and Leah looked at each other, shrugged, and got up. "Come on," said Christina as the lights started to dim. "Let's get this over with so we can get back."

The kids were the only ones in the casbah of great tufted sofas, huge highback chairs, pedestals, plants, and exotic curtained cubbyholes and corridors.

"At least the bathrooms are normal," said Grant, skulking out of the men's restroom.

"You would expect to see a cloak and dagger somewhere," said Leah.

"Cloak and dagger, cloak and dagger," chanted Grant in a creepy voice. He hunched over and pretended to hold the end of a cloak up to his face with one hand, while he clutched a dagger in the other. Soon, all four kids were slithering around the tufted sofas and down the exotic curtained corridors of the Fox Theatre's lower level, doing their cloak and dagger dance. Until—

From one of the cubbyholes, a figure stepped out in front of them, wearing a dark billowing cloak and a black mask over the eyes like Zorro wore.

The kids let out a collective gasp and stood very still, as though waiting for something. Christina could hear in the near distance the deep drone of speech, then low chords of music, and the muffled sound of applause. The dark corridor lightened as a door must have opened and the cheering became louder. Someone entered the corridor, and the door slammed shut.

"Where are they?" a voice demanded from behind them.

"Over here," said the man's voice behind the mask.

"Did you grill them?"

Grant's eyes flew wide open. "Cook us?" he mouthed to Christina. Christina shook her head "no" and put her arms around all of the kids.

"Look, kid," the cloak pointed to Grant. "You've got a piece of paper we need real bad. If you give it to us, we'll take you all back to your seats. And we won't bother you again."

The man behind the children, whose voice was as smooth as a radio announcer's, added in feigned friendliness, "We don't know where you got it. Maybe just off the street or from a table. We don't care how. We'd just like to have it back."

"We really don't know what you mean," Christina said shakily.

"We're talking to him," said the cloak, pointing to Grant.

Grant broke away from Christina's grasp and walked forward. "The only note I had was my homework," said Grant, his voice trembling. "But someone took that away from me."

"They must've figured..." the cloak began, and then fell silent.

"That's the only note they took?" the smooth voice asked eagerly.

"Yes," Grant insisted.

There was a long silence.

Then Grant remembered. "Oh yeah..." he started.

"Oh yeah what, kid...oh yeah what?" said the cloak.

"Let him talk, fool!" said the smooth voice in a loud whisper.

"Probably a lie he's made up real quick," said the cloak.

"Hush!" thundered the voice.

Hurriedly, Grant went on. "Oh, yeah, I did have another note. I found it in an elevator."

"Well, give it to us, please," said the voice, all butter and honey once more.

Again, the dead silence. Then Grant said, "But I don't have it anymore."

"What?" both men said together.

"It's in a big wire wastebasket near a pretzel stand," cried Grant.

The cloak laughed an evil laugh. "Great, kid!" he said. "There's only a million trash cans in this city. And pretzel vendors move every two minutes."

"Shut up," the voice warned. "Think!" he demanded.

"It was downtown, near Five Points and a bus stop," said Grant. "You can tell the note from the rest of the trash cause I wiped mustard off my mouth with it."

"Mustard?" the men repeated. They sounded like they were breathing double time. "Pretzel mustard," admitted Grant.

The men laughed. There was one "schwoo" of relief.

"But we still can't—" the cloak began to argue.

"Yes, we can!" the voice said, sharper than a dagger. "Get back to your show, kids."

8
HOT DOUGHNUTS AND SECRETS

The big neon "HOT NOW" sign was lit up and flashing on the Krispy Kreme store front when Papa, Mimi, and the kids left the Fox Theatre. That meant the soft, tasty doughnuts were fresh out of the oven. Papa could not resist turning into the famous landmark with its green tile roof and massive road sign.

The kids perched on four stools, watching doughnut after doughnut travel down the conveyor belt. Grant looked over his shoulder at Mimi and Papa, deep in conversation at a table across the room.

"I felt like falling down and bawling," he said, stuffing another warm, chewy doughnut into his mouth. Pieces of glaze clung to his nose.

"You were really brave, little brother," said Christina, putting her arm around him.

"You were great!" said Philip. "I was scared to death. I never could have talked to those guys, especially the one in the mask. Hi-five, man!"

Grant licked his fingers. The two boys stood up, smacking their right hands together and kicking up one back leg.

"Who in the world were those men?" asked Leah, reaching for another irresistible doughnut. "Why would anyone go to that much trouble for a piece of paper with numbers on it?"

Christina stared at one doughnut as it came out of the oven and wobbled along the conveyor belt. It landed nicely into a large box with the green and red Krispy Kreme logo. "You know, I just feel like it's all connected," she said.

"What's all connected?" said Grant, eyeing his sister suspiciously.

"That note you found ... those evil guys at the Fox ... maybe even the bus hijacking. I just feel that they are all connected in some way to Mr. Black Trenchcoat and his mustard-colored Mustang."

"Look, Christina," said Grant seriously. "I like a mystery as much as you do. Well, maybe I don't like it quite as much as you do!" he said, rolling his eyes and giggling. "But these are scary dudes. I'm glad I threw that dumb piece of paper away. Let them go off and find their stupid note and leave us alone. We don't have to deal with them anymore."

"It's not quite that easy, Grant," said Christina.

Christina stared nervously at Grant as she reached deep into her jeans pocket. Slowly, she pulled out the piece of paper that he had thrown away.

"I'm sorry," she said. "I swiped it out of the trash. I have a funny feeling about it."

Leah, Philip, and Grant stared in disbelief.

9
PILLOW FIGHTS AND CONGA LINES

The next morning, a candy apple sun beamed into the living area of Mimi and Papa's twelfth floor room at the Westin Peachtree Plaza. Grant and Philip were sacked out in their sleeping bags. Leah was quietly reading a new mystery she had bought at Underground the day before.

Christina's pen hovered over a sheet of fancy hotel stationery. At the top of her page, she had written the word "Clues." The list included most of the strange things that had happened during the last twenty-four hours. She hoped that by writing them down, the mystery might become clearer.

As she wrote, she watched the shafts of sunlight stripe the capitol dome. Workmen were already plastered to its convex side, doing whatever they were doing to it.

Suddenly, she was swatted in the back of the head with a pillow. "Cloak and dagger! Cloak and dagger!" Grant's squeaky, half-awake voice intoned.

"Ouch," she yelled. "Does that make you feel better, Grant?" she asked when she realized who it was.

"Yeah, it does!" yelled Grant. He swatted her again.

Christina grabbed the pillow and swatted back. "Cut it out!" she cried.

"Just kidding," Grant said. Then he struck her again with the pillow she had dropped.

"Hey, you guys," said Leah. "Stop with the pillows!"

"Where are Mimi and Papa?" Grant asked, turning to Leah.

"They went down to get some coffee," replied Leah.

Grant turned back to Christina. "I dreamed about cloaks and daggers and mean men all night. I'm plumb wore out." He socked her again with the pillow.

"You?" said Christina. "If you had given that note back in the first place, none of this would be happening."

"What were you going to do, Christina?" asked Grant. "Why didn't you just give them the note? What if they had hurt me?" Grant whacked her again with the pillow.

"Whoa! What's going on?" asked Philip, coming into the room and rubbing his eyes. "I was dreaming that some guy in a Zorro mask was dueling it out at the Krispy Kreme with Brer Rabbit."

Everyone began to laugh at the thought of such a **melodrama**.

"You must have dreamed that because we're going to the Wren's Nest today," said Leah, shaking her chocolate-brown curls.

"Or maybe, I dreamed it because some guy in a mask scared the living daylights out of me last night," cried Philip. He ran around the room, doing their "cloak and dagger" dance.

"There we were," said Grant, forming a cloak and dagger conga line behind Philip, "minding our own business...when... when...POW...the real thing appears!!!"

"I'm just glad he didn't have a dagger!" cried Leah. She jumped up and joined the conga line.

Christina ran across the room and grabbed Grant by the shoulders. "Grant, I would never let anyone hurt you. I would have given them the note if I thought that was going to happen. I am so—"

Just then, the doorknob turned and in walked Mimi and Papa.

"What's going on here?" said Mimi. "We're due at the Wren's Nest in an hour, and then we're going to CNN. You still need to eat breakfast, so get a move on!"

Ten minutes later, the kids were galloping down the hall toward the elevator.

"Can't miss some pancakes and whipped cream," yelled Grant.

"Waffles for me!" Philip sang.

"Hurry, the elevator doors are closing!" yelled Christina, catching up with the boys. The four ran pell-mell to the elevator and reached it just in time to catch a glimpse of a black trench coat as the door swooshed shut in front of them.

10
A WREN'S NEST AND A YELLOW MUSTANG

"This is a cool old house," said Leah, as the kids walked from the back yard around to the front of the Wren's Nest.

They had just listened to a storyteller relate the story of Brer Rabbit and the Tar Baby. Mimi was inside researching Joel Chandler Harris, who had lived in the house long ago. He was an Atlanta newspaper columnist who wrote down stories he had heard as a boy about Brer Rabbit.

"Now, who was Uncle Remus?" asked Philip.

"He was the character that Joel Chandler Harris created to tell the stories of Brer Rabbit," replied Christina.

"My school class came up here a couple years ago," said Leah. "We learned that most of the Brer Rabbit stories originated in Africa. In America, slaves told and retold the tales. Mr. Harris heard them as a boy and wrote them down so everyone could read them."

"And he lived here?" asked Grant.

"That's right," replied Christina. "He named this house 'The Wren's Nest' because a family of little wrens set up housekeeping in his mailbox."

"Cool," said Grant, dancing around. "I wonder if the birds pooped on the mail."

Everyone giggled. "I'm pretty sure the postman stopped putting mail in the mailbox," said Christina. "At least until the bird eggs were hatched and the baby birds were gone."

Just then, the kids got to the front of the house. They stopped cold in their tracks. There sat a mustard-yellow Mustang on the street in front of the house! The car was empty, but coming down the steps of the Wren's Nest behind them was Mr. Black Trenchcoat.

"Well, hello!" said Mr. Trenchcoat. "Didn't we meet the other day?"

No one answered.

"Bye, now," he said, walking to his car. "Gotta get back to work." When he reached the door of his car, he turned. "Need a lift?"

"Yeah," Philip said, eyeing the snazzy car.

"No!" shouted Christina. "Our grandparents are with us. Thanks, anyway."

With a nod, he got in the car and drove off.

"I thought this mystery was over," said Grant, scowling at Christina.

The kids walked as if in a trance up the steps to the wide front porch of The Wren's Nest.

Grant broke the silence. "Look, there's the mailbox," he said, walking over to it. He glanced at Christina. "Great place to hide a clue."

It would be a great place, thought Christina. She walked over and slowly opened the little mailbox hanging on the wall of the house. There was nothing, but Christina still wondered what was up with Mr. Black Trenchcoat.

11
NEWS FLASH!

CNN was bustling with activity. For the 24-hour cable news network, it was just another day of world news. For Christina, it was a dream come true.

This is so exciting she thought. *I've always wanted to visit CNN.* She bounced off the towering escalator that transported them up into the CNN news production facility.

"Awesome! We're inside the world," said Grant. He flung his arms wide open as they stepped into a room shaped like a globe. "Look at all this cool news stuff! Do you think we'll be on TV, Mimi?"

"I wonder if we'll see some on-air anchors," said Christina. She happily looked all around.

"What's an 'on-air-an-ker'?" asked Grant.

"It's a person who reports the news live on the television," replied Christina.

"I've arranged for you to take a tour," said Mimi. "Keep your eyes open. You never know who you'll see. I'll be back soon." She left them with their tour guide.

On their tour, the kids learned about big news events CNN had covered over the years. They sat in a replica of a CNN control room and watched a lady direct a newscast. From behind a huge, glass-enclosed balcony, they looked out into the CNN newsroom for a bird's eye view of the action.

"Who are all those people?" asked Leah.

"Producers, writers, reporters, and technicians," replied their guide. "They all help get the news from the source to your television screen."

The guide led them into a studio set with a camera, news desk, and monitors. He looked at his watch. "You stay right here. I'll be back in a minute," he said, closing the door.

Grant scurried behind the news desk. He started playing with switches under the desk.

Christina noticed a red neon sign light up over the door. It flashed the words "ON AIR." Suddenly, the row of television monitors in the room went from CNN's current news program—to Grant. Her little brother was on the screen!

Christina looked out the huge picture window overlooking the newsroom below. She saw Grant's picture pop up on dozens of monitors. People frantically pointed at the screens. Alarms beeped. Heads spun around and up. Within seconds, hundreds of people were staring at the kids in the studio!

Christina's face turned red with embarrassment. "Grant, you're on the air!" she cried.

"I am?" asked Grant, his eyes wide. In his best newscaster voice, he quipped, "Today, the weather will be cloudy with a chance of meatballs." Grant mugged straight into the camera.

Christina ran over and pulled Grant away from the camera. The studio door swung open. The guide and Mimi rushed in.

"GRANT!" cried Mimi, shaking her finger at him.

Perspiration poured down the distraught guide's face. He quickly flipped several switches under the desk. CNN's current program came back on the air. Still grumbling about the interruption, the people in the newsroom turned back to their business of reporting about the world.

Christina covered her face with her hands.

"Don't worry, Christina," said Grant, "you can have my autograph! Now, I'm an 'on-air-an-ker'!"

The guide hurriedly ushered the group out of CNN. No one saw the dark figure slide down the hallway and narrow staircases not far behind them.

12
WATCH OUT FOR THE MUSTARD!

Grant buckled the strap on his black and silver helmet. He stood at the top of the long, straight ramp that led to the front door of the High Museum of Art. The building's white and glass cube architecture gleamed against the brilliant blue sky.

"Watch out!" screamed Grant. "Here I come!"

"You better hurry, Grant," yelled Christina. "Mimi is going to walk out any minute and see you."

With that, Grant hopped on his skateboard and began his descent.

WHOOSH!

"I'm flying now!" yelled Grant.

Just then, a deliveryman started up the long ramp. He was pushing cases of old-fashioned Coke bottles stacked on a hand truck.

"Watch out!" yelled Philip. He covered his face with his hands and peeked through his fingers.

"GRANT!" yelled Christina. "Be careful!"

Grant hunched down on his skateboard and swerved to his right around the delivery cart. The deliveryman lost his balance and nearly fell. But he managed to save his bottles of Coke by throwing up his arms and balancing the top case. Grant continued to skim along the ramp's white railing. At the end of the ramp, he swerved back to his left and made a perfect stop in front of the three kids.

"That was perfecto!" yelled Philip, uncovering his eyes.

"That was *close* is what that was," added Leah, zipping up her green jacket.

"Sorry!" yelled Christina to the deliveryman. "He's a showoff!"

"Did you see the colas on that guy's cart?" asked Grant excitedly. "The bottles had

YELLOW Coke in them. They looked like Coke bottles filled with mustard!"

Christina looked back at the scowling deliveryman, just as Mimi walked around him and his hand truck.

"Let's go!" Mimi called. "We're off to another location. Grant, I hope you're being careful on that thing!"

Grant hopped back on his skateboard and followed everyone down the sidewalk. Christina looked over her shoulder at the deliveryman, who continued to stare at them.

Mustard-yellow Coke, she thought. *What is that all about?* And then her stomach flipped. *Mustard. Why do I keep hearing about mustard? And why does that deliveryman seem so creepy?*

13
FLYING THROUGH THE TREETOPS

The wind was starting to pick up. The wispy white clouds of the afternoon were thickening and turning grey. Mimi and the kids walked briskly through Piedmont Park, Atlanta's well-known, 100-year-old park.

"I love this place," said Mimi, stopping to look at the downtown skyline rising over the tree-lined park. "It's no time to tarry, though."

"What's that mean?" asked Philip.

"It means to take longer than you should," said Mimi. "So let's keep going!"

The kids took turns putting on Grant's helmet and maneuvering the paths on his skateboard, then, waiting for the entourage to catch up.

"Want a turn, Mimi?" asked Grant, pulling his green sock cap out of his jacket pocket.

"I think I'll pass," said Mimi, pointing to her red high heels. "Remind me to wear my tennis shoes next time. Here's the Botanical Garden entrance. I don't know how long this will take. I'll text you when I'm done. Be sure to check out the Canopy Walk. It's that way!" Mimi pointed to the right and walked into the visitor's center. She turned back around abruptly and yelled, "NO skateboarding, Grant!"

Grant shot an arm straight up with a "thumbs up." The kids took off down a path lined by woods and beautiful gardens.

"Look at all the plants blooming in the winter," said Leah.

"This brochure says the garden has something in flower year-round," Christina said.

"What's 'in-the-flower'?" asked Grant, peering into a mass of blooming plants.

"'In flower' means the plant is blooming," said Christina, turning around to look at him.

Then, something caught her eye. Two scruffy-looking men stood near a clump of trees. They stared straight at the kids. When the men realized Christina was looking back, they quickly turned away.

"Let's go to the Canopy Walk," Christina suggested. The Canopy Walk is a wide concrete walkway. It winds through the treetops of Storza Woods, one of the last mature hardwood forests in Atlanta.

"I feel like I'm floating through the trees," sang Leah. She danced and pirouetted as the kids followed the path. Below, the gardens put on quite a show of winter color.

Christina kept her eye on the two men as they entered the Canopy Walk behind the kids. She thought they were following them. But were they?

"Let's go over to the Children's Garden," she said as they exited the Canopy Walk. *This is a test*, she thought. *Let's see if they follow us over here.*

The men sauntered behind, always within sight of Christina. *If I can see them, then they can see me*, she thought.

"Look at those waterfalls," cried Grant, his voice rising over the low hum of the water. "We need to come back and play in there next summer."

"How about now?" said Philip, running toward the falls with Grant close behind.

"OK, you guys!" yelled Leah. "I think Ms. Marsh would notice that you're wet!"

"And cold," added Christina. At this point, she had a **palpable** sense that the men were staring a hole straight into her back.

At the children's garden, the kids crossed the Flower Bridge and whipped down the slide at the Treehouse. They scampered through the Butterfly Maze and around the Sunflower Fountain, wishing it were summer. All the time, Christina kept watch of the men who slowly strolled behind them.

The sun was starting to sink behind the tall buildings of Atlanta. The low, wintry clouds that were slowly rolling in were making the garden even darker. There were few other people around—except for the two men.

"Let's head back toward the visitor's center," said Christina. "Mimi's bound to be done soon." She looked over her shoulder and saw that the men were closer—much closer. She felt the urge to run.

"We need to get out of here," she said quietly to the others. "Let's run."

"What's wrong?" asked Grant.

Christina cocked her head in the direction of the men. With one look, the four kids took off.

So did the men.

"We can outrun these guys," said Leah. "Stick with me!"

"Can you run fast?" asked Christina.

Leah just smiled—and took off—quick as a bunny.

With Leah in the lead, the pace picked up. Christina could no longer see the men, but they had to keep going. At Storza Woods, Grant yelled, "Let's split up! You go through the woods!" He took off for the Canopy Walk.

Oh no, thought Christina, panting. *Now I have to worry about two men possibly chasing us, AND Grant skateboarding the Canopy Walk. Mimi won't like this.*

As Leah, Philip, and Christina darted around the trees, they could hear the swish of Grant's skateboard above their heads.

Then, it was over as suddenly as it had begun. The three runners reached the visitor's center. Within seconds, Grant jumped a park bench and stopped beside them.

"WHOOOHOOO!" he yelled. "That was one great way to see the treetops! I felt like a squirrel!"

Grant handed Christina a sheet of paper. "I swooped it up at the end of the canopy walkway," he said. The kids read the paper over her shoulder.

"It's a campaign flyer," said Christina.

"The guy who dropped the piece of paper in the elevator," said Grant, "was wearing a button that said the same thing."

Just then, Mimi walked out of the visitor's center. "Great! There you are," she said. "I was just ready to text you."

"I'm famished, Mimi," said Grant.

"Good!" she replied. "We're going someplace where you can eat a whole lot of good, Southern-style vegetables."

"Vegetables!" Grant and Philip moaned in unison. "UUUUGH!"

"BRRRR," said Mimi. "It's really getting chilly." She took a red plaid scarf out of her bag and tied it around her neck. "I hear there is winter weather headed this way. Let's go!"

The group took off walking. Christina looked back into the garden. *Are those two men beside the trees*, she thought, *or just the shadows of Storza Woods?*

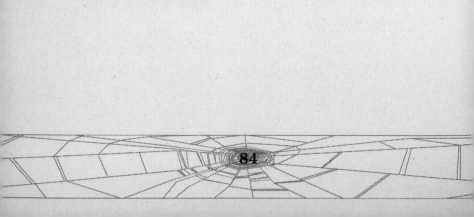

84

14
MUSTANG STAKEOUT

Christina placed a forkful of steaming chicken and dumplings in her mouth. She surveyed the big dining room at Mary Mac's Tea Room. There were no scruffy guys and no Mr. Black Trenchcoat in sight. It was just a room packed with happy diners. Tables were filled with fried chicken, black-eyed peas, cheese grits, collard greens, fried green tomatoes, Georgia peach cobbler, and banana pudding.

Yum, thought Christina. *I'm glad we're not being chased in here.*

"Why do they call this place a tea room?" Christina asked Mimi.

"A lady named Mary McKenzie opened it in 1945," replied Mimi. "She was a good Southern cook, and she needed an income.

Back then, women couldn't just open up their own restaurant. It wasn't considered 'lady-like.' So, she called it a tea room to make it sound more refined."

"Did you eat here when you were a girl, Ms. Marsh?" asked Leah.

"I sure did," said Mimi, looking out the large picture window next to their table. "I remember when trolley cars clanged up and down this street. There were big tents set up, serving ice-cold watermelon. The Atlanta Crackers used to play baseball on a field just down the street."

"CRACKERS?" said Grant. He licked fried chicken crust from his fingers. "What kind of crackers play baseball?"

Papa set down his big glass of sweet tea. "The Crackers was Atlanta's minor league team before the Braves came here," he said. "They were a fun team to watch."

"Papa, let's talk to the owner while the kids finish up," said Mimi.

As soon as Mimi and Papa were gone, Christina pulled out her list of clues. "We need to discuss this," she said.

Grant said, "I've been watching for mean men ever since we sat down."

"And black trench coats," said Leah.

"And yellow Mustangs," added Philip, glancing out the window.

"There are a lot of weird things going on," said Christina. "I think it's all connected. There's a mystery here. We just don't understand it yet. First, a man wearing a BE AWARE, VOTE O'HARE button drops a note in the elevator. Grant picks it up. Next, another man demands that Grant give him the note."

"But I gave him my homework," said Grant. He and Philip started to giggle.

"Then, I get that fortune at Underground," said Christina, "and we meet Mr. Black Trenchcoat."

"Then, our bus gets hijacked," added Leah.

"And Mr. Black Trenchcoat shows up and helps me," said Grant.

"How about the creepy men at the Fox Theatre?" said Philip.

"We keep spotting Mr. Black Trenchcoat and his Mustang everywhere," added Christina.

"Then those guys chase us through the gardens," said Leah.

"But they couldn't catch us!" said Grant. He and Philip started singing and wiggling their bodies, "Oh, yeah. Oh, yeah!"

"And Grant finds a flyer that says, BE AWARE, VOTE O'HARE," Christina says, folding up her paper. "Well, whether we like it or not, we have a mystery."

She looked around the restaurant again. *Still no scruffy men or black trench coats*, she thought.

But just then, Philip's jaw dropped. The other three kids followed his gaze out the window to see a yellow Mustang slowly passing by.

15

A CLOSE CALL

"You know," said Grant, "I've decided that looking at 'gi-gan-ti-ca' dinosaurs in an almost-dark museum creeps me out! Can't they turn some lights on?"

The kids were roaming around the Fernbank Museum of Natural History after hours, while Mimi interviewed the curator.

They now stood in the museum's Great Hall. Huge replicas of some of the largest dinosaurs ever unearthed in the world stood poised for battle. A flock of twenty-one prehistoric birds hovered overhead, as if reacting to the commotion of the battle.

"Holy cow!" said Philip. "This looks like the real thing."

"UURRAAAAAAHH!" roared Grant. Everybody jumped.

"Grant! That wasn't funny," said Christina, starting to laugh in spite of herself.

"What do you mean?" said Grant. "It was hysterical. You should have seen the looks on your faces." He started laughing so hard that he backed into a fossilized crocodile, fell, and bumped his head. The kids started laughing.

"Ouch!" Grant said, rubbing his head. "Now, THAT wasn't funny."

Just then, they heard a creak and a loud bang. A shaft of light came from the direction of the lobby. "Let's go that way," said Grant. "I need some light."

As they walked, they could see that the light was coming from the concession area. A man was stocking Coca-Cola behind a counter.

"Grant," said Leah, "that is the same deliveryman you ran into with your skateboard!" Grant's mouth flew open. "He's also the same man who snatched my homework away from me," he said. "I didn't recognize him before."

"Holy cow, you're right," whispered Philip.

"Shush!" said Christina. "Get down."

They hunched down behind some chairs and tables. Four sets of eyes peered at the deliveryman stacking Coke cases.

"UUUGH," said Grant. "Mr. Snatch has some of that yucky-looking yellow Coke."

Christina spied a piece of paper on the floor and scooted over to pick it up.

"What's that?" asked Leah as Christina opened it up.

48 bottles = 672,000

"I don't know," said Christina, "but I bet he dropped it."

BANG! Grant knocked over a chair.

The deliveryman's head jerked up. He stared into the darkening dining area. "What are you kids doing here this time of night?" he said nicely. Then, his eyes adjusted to the darkness. "Hey, I know you," he said menacingly. In an instant, he jumped over the counter, out of the light and into the darkness. Like an arrow shot, he aimed straight at the kids.

The kids took off with Leah in the lead. She ran like a possessed bullet straight into the main area of the lobby, nearly running into Mimi, Papa, and the curator.

"Are you all right?" asked the curator. "You look like you've seen a ghost."

"We're OK," said Christina, bringing up the rear. "We just got a little spooked by the dinosaurs in the dark."

"Yes, they can be a little unnerving after dark," said the curator. "Come back during the day, Ms. Marsh, and bring these charming children with you," he added, leading them to the door.

Christina looked over her shoulder but saw no one in the pitch-black corridor. But a shiver ran down her spine. She felt like someone was watching them from the darkness.

16

LIGHTNING BOLTS AND A CRUISING CAR

Grant slouched in the overstuffed chair in the hotel room. He stared out the window at the capitol building in the distance. The capitol dome was now the color of rusty autumn leaves against glowering clouds. Lightning ripped tears in the dark sky, and a downpour followed.

"Boy, that dome is looking worse instead of better," he commented to no one in particular. Leah raised her head but went straight back to her mystery book. Philip was wrapped up in his sleeping bag, immersed in watching his favorite cartoons on TV.

Christina sauntered in, combing her straight brown hair. "Wow, a storm is cool from up here," she said. She walked over to where Grant sat staring out the window.

"Have you seen it again?" she asked Grant.

"Yeah, two more times," he replied. "It drove by real slow, then went that way. A little later, it did the same thing again. Do you think it's the same car? There could be more than one, you know."

Philip turned around. "I've never seen an old, yellow Mustang before," he said. "I'd love to ride in it."

"Yeah, I got the feeling it's Mr. Black Trenchcoat, too," said Christina.

Just then, Mimi bustled into the room. "OK, everyone," she said. "We have a full agenda today. Wear your rain gear, but take a heavy jacket because it's supposed to turn colder."

Christina slung her backpack over her shoulder and looked down at the street below. Then she spotted it. Even in the rain, she was sure it was the yellow Mustang cruising by before turning in the direction of the state capitol.

"Ka-pow!" A sudden bolt of lightning and thunder shook the big window. Christina jumped back and clutched her backpack. "But why?" she said in a half whisper. "Why?"

17
PANDA ESCAPE

Mimi and the kids were at the Atlanta Cyclorama. They had watched a short movie about the Civil War. Now, they pondered the famous panoramic painting. Believed to be the world's largest painting, it depicts the 1864 Battle of Atlanta. During the battle, Confederate troops desperately tried to save Atlanta from the Union army. At the base of the painting is a model, or diorama, of the battle with three-dimensional figures and terrain. It looks like an extension of the painting.

"It's like a 3D movie," said Christina. "I feel like I'm in the middle of the bloody mess. I can almost smell the smoke!"

"I can't tell where the figures in the front end and the painting begins," said Leah, peering at the scene.

Christina had studied the Civil War and the Battle of Atlanta in school. Brother had killed brother in the awful battle. The city had burned to the ground. *But like the great mythical bird, the phoenix,* she thought, *Atlanta rose from the ashes.*

"This scene actually took place very close to where we are now," said Mimi.

"What?" cried Grant incredulously. "You mean all these dead bodies and horses and cannons—and blood—were right around here?"

"I know the war was terrible," said Leah, "but I'm glad it led to the end of slavery in America." She looked from Mimi back to the painting.

"Yes," said Mimi, putting an arm around Leah's shoulders. "The Civil War helped to change some big things that were wrong in our country."

Back outside, the group headed next door to the Zoo Atlanta entrance. Mimi purchased bags of peanuts for everyone. "I'm leaving you here," she said. "I'll text when I'm done. Don't eat too much, Grant."

"Mmmrrhha, mmmrrhha," Grant said. His mouth was already stuffed with peanuts.

"Let's go see the giant pandas," said Christina, shelling a peanut. "They're this way."

"I'm glad I don't live in a zoo," said Grant as they walked. "Nothing belongs in a cage."

Suddenly, Grant stopped. He whispered, "Except maybe Snatch over there—in a jail cage."

There was the deliveryman again—the man who had snatched Grant's homework! He was looking straight at the kids. He gave them a bold, evil grin and moved their way.

The four took off running. They threaded their way through the crowd until they came to a dead end. Ignoring the POSITIVELY NO ADMITTANCE sign, Christina shoved open a heavy door. The kids ducked to get inside. She bolted the door behind them.

They had entered a dark and narrow hallway. Light filtered in from a small opening in the side wall just ahead. Christina gestured for them to follow her. Cautiously, she crouched toward the light. Then, she lowered her head to see where the opening led. *Things can't get much worse*, Christina thought. But all at once, she was eyeball to eyeball with a monstrous, hairy, black and white panda bear!

The panda had just finished showing off for dozens of gawkers outside his home. Now, he was coming in to rest. Petrified, Christina and the kids backed against the hall wall as the panda entered the tunnel. When the panda saw them, his eyes popped wide open.

The huge bear started to lumber toward them. Four kids gasped in unison. *Why did I come down this way?* thought Christina. She tried to move but was frozen in her tracks.

Suddenly, a shaft of light flooded in from another door a few feet away. As the panda's paw brushed against the tip of Christina's nose, a frantic voice shouted, "This way, kids!" Grant yanked Christina's arm and pulled her head first out into the sunshine.

As she scrambled to her feet, Christina saw the tail end of a black trench coat flap around the corner of the building.

18
GIANT PANDA SOUL FOOD

Mimi and the kids walked out onto Auburn Avenue, one of the most historic African American streets in America.

"Best soul food I ever ate," said Philip, patting his tummy.

"Why do they call it soul food?" asked Grant.

"It's just a word we use for African American cuisine," said Philip.

"What's quee-zeen?" asked Grant.

"FOOD!" replied Philip. "Soul food makes you feel good. And it makes you FULL!"

Mimi and the girls laughed as they walked down the street.

"This neighborhood is called Sweet Auburn," said Mimi. "It's where Martin Luther

King, Jr., was born, raised, lived, worked, and worshiped. It's also where he is buried. Much of Sweet Auburn is now part of the Martin Luther King, Jr., National Historic Site."

The group stopped and looked at the small house where Dr. King was born. Then, they walked to the National Park Service visitor's center.

"Look around," said Mimi. "I'm going in here for a few minutes."

Soon they were giggling about their near-catastrophe in the panda cage.

"Did you see the look on Christina's face?" said Grant, striking a horrified pose.

"I was too busy crying," said Leah.

"I can't even blame it on the guy chasing us," said Christina. "That was my own doing. And I guess Mr. Black Trenchcoat helped us out because he thinks we still have the note."

"Yeah, it would be pretty hard to get that note from you," said Grant, "if you were in the BELLY OF A GIANT PANDA! Just think, Christina, you were almost Giant Panda Soul Food!"

Grant flopped onto a wooden park bench and doubled over laughing. Then, he jumped up and said seriously, "Do you think they went through all the trash cans downtown and know we have it?"

"I don't know," said Christina. She fingered the notes in her pocket and looked over her shoulder. "But now, we have two notes."

No one noticed Mr. Black Trenchcoat watching them from another park bench on Auburn Avenue.

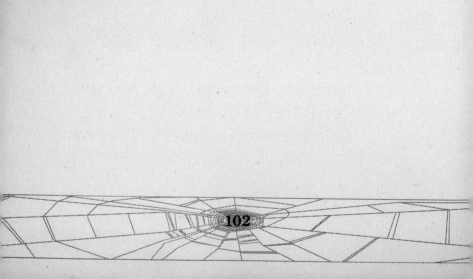

19

SNATCH'S YELLOW COKE!

The four kids huddled around a kiosk in a brightly colored room at The World of Coca-Cola. Atlanta is the headquarters for Coca-Cola. The World of Coca-Cola is the soft drink company's huge, interactive museum.

The kids had already explored several floors of exhibits. They had learned about the history of Coke. Now, they were sampling the 60 different Coke products sold in other countries.

"Taste it, taste it!" said Grant to Christina. "It's yummy!"

Christina looked suspiciously at Grant. "Are you sure?" she said warily.

"It's my favorite," he said, batting his eyelashes.

Christina pulled the lever, filled a sample cup, and tasted. "YUCK!!" she yelled. She spit the liquid back into her cup. "That's terrible. It tastes like licorice!"

Grant and Philip danced around. "I knew I could get her to taste it," sang Grant.

"Funny, funny!" said Christina, walking away from the kiosk.

Grant and Philip danced and high-fived as they followed the girls to a soda-fountain style counter. Several attendants were serving samples of American Coke products.

"This is more like it," said Christina. She took a sip of Diet Coke.

Suddenly, Grant reached behind the counter and pulled out a glass Coke bottle. Quick as a wink, he unscrewed the cap and put the bottle up to his lips.

"Hold on there, fella!" the attendant said. He politely grabbed the bottle away from Grant. "You can't have one of these. That's a new flavor. We can't release it for a few more days. Until then, NO ONE can taste it."

Christina whirled around in time to see the attendant place the glass bottle of yellow

Coke under the counter. It was just like the bottles they had seen Snatch, the deliveryman, delivering all over town.

"Sorry," said Grant. He screwed up his mouth and face. "YUCK!" He wiped the yellow liquid from his lips with a napkin. "Good luck with that stuff. It tastes and smells horrible. I don't feel so good." He threw his napkin away in disgust.

Christina stared at the cases of yellow Coke stacked behind the counter. Something was very strange about the whole situation. But what?

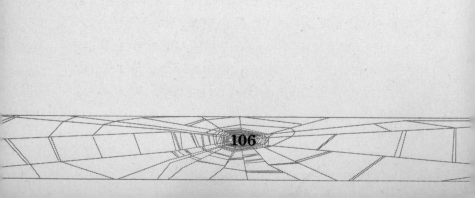

20

ROBBERS AND INDIANS!

Christina, Grant, Leah, and Philip stood in front of the picture window in their room at the Westin Peachtree Plaza with frowns on their faces. A blanket of grey, wintry clouds covered the once-blue sky.

"It looks cold out there," said Christina. "Even the workmen are leaving," said Grant, pressing his nose to the window. "That gold dome looks worse than when they started."

"It doesn't seem very bright for all that cleaning," said Leah. "I think it was shinier before."

"Aw, it's just the clouds," said Christina. "Nothing looks bright on a grey day like this."

Just then, Mimi entered the room, tying a red wool scarf around her neck. "We're off to Stone Mountain this morning," she said.

"Bundle up! While I work, you might want to ride some rides. There's a high-speed Swiss cable car that goes to the top of the mountain. It's called the Summit Skyride."

By the time Mimi, Papa, and the kids got to Stone Mountain, a bone-chilling wind was blowing around the gigantic rock that rose just east of Atlanta. Stone Mountain is the largest piece of exposed granite in the world. Carved deep into its face is a sculpture larger than a football field. The sculpture shows three Confederate heroes: Confederate President Jefferson Davis, General Robert E. Lee, and General Stonewall Jackson.

"It looks like an iceberg to me," said Grant, as the kids stood in the parking lot staring up at Stone Mountain.

"People say more of it is underground than above—just like a real iceberg," said Mimi, waving goodbye to them. "It's just the tip of the iceberg!"

"Kind of like this mystery," Christina muttered, putting on her gloves. "Let's take the scenic railroad train ride."

The kids bought tickets at the train terminal and climbed aboard the first car. The steam engine belched puffs of white smoke into puffs of white clouds. A whistle shrilled. With jerks and jolts, the train lurched forward and picked up speed. It settled into the rusty clackety-clack of wheel-to-track as it began its five-mile excursion around the mountain.

The train streaked through narrow tunnels of pines, flickering ice crystals. The conductor kept up an animated chatter about the olden days. Deep in the woods, the train slowed.

"Why are we stopping?" the conductor asked. He looked around frantically and motioned to the passengers to hush.

The kids laughed, suspecting what was to come. Sure enough, out of the trees stormed horses mounted by actors dressed as cowboy robbers and Indians ready to stage a train robbery.

It was great! Savages ran up and down the aisles bellowing and brandishing hatchets over everyone's heads. They surrounded the seats in a frenzied war dance.

Then it happened.

The mask that one of the cowboys was wearing slipped down so his face was visible. It was the deliveryman!

"Snatch!" yelled Grant.

The four kids jumped off the train and plunged into the frozen forest of Stone Mountain. The icy underbrush crackled under their boots. The bitter wind whipped their faces as they thrashed their way through low-hanging limbs.

"Look!" called Grant, pointing to a sign marking a trail up Stone Mountain. "They can't follow us on horses if we climb up the mountain."

"Let's go!" shouted Leah, taking off. The kids began to climb the backside of Stone Mountain. The trail was steep but well marked.

When they had almost reached the top, Grant turned around to see cowboys and Indians down below. "They're going to see us!" he yelled at Christina. Christina pointed to a small park maintenance shed in some woods off to the side of the trail.

"In here," she said, panting from the steep climb. She pushed open the door, and the kids snuck into the small hut.

"What are we gonna do now?" Grant pleaded.

"I know you're scared," said Christina. "I'll figure out something." She peeked through the cracks of the shed walls. "Look! We're almost on top of the mountain. I can see the Summit Skyride ticket booth. If we can get there, we can buy a ticket down and get away from those guys."

Christina turned back around. As her eyes adjusted to the darkness of the shed, she saw Grant staring at dozens of cases of the new yellow Coke.

"This stuff is everywhere," he said. He stuck out his tongue and made a gagging gesture.

Christina reached down and picked up a piece of paper from the shed's concrete floor.

World of Coke – 100 cases

Zoo Atlanta – 50 cases

Fernbank – 30 cases

Clump, clump! Christina heard the sound of horses' hooves outside the shed. She jerked back around and peered through the cracks in the shed. There in the clearing were the robbers and Indians.

"It's Snatch again," said Grant.

"There's the bus-jacker," whispered Leah.

"That's the voices of The Mask and Mr. Smooth Voice, too," said Christina. "We need to get out of here!"

She lifted a crowbar from a shelf. As quietly as possible, she wedged the crowbar between a couple of rotten boards on the back of the shed. Grant and Philip stacked the pieces in a corner. When the opening was large enough, the four slipped out.

Keeping the shack between them and the men, the kids sneaked through the trees to the Skyride. People were boarding the blue cable car as the kids jumped in line to buy a ticket.

"I hope they don't sell out of tickets," said Grant, looking around nervously. More people arrived behind them, and the kids felt a little safer.

The line inched forward. "This is taking FOREVER!" Grant moaned.

Finally, Christina purchased four tickets. The ticket agent said, "That's all, folks. Next lift leaves to go down the mountain in 30 minutes."

With a groan, the rest of the people walked away, leaving the kids exposed.

Just then, Snatch, now wearing regular clothes, spotted them and came running.

"Hurry! Everyone get on board," said Christina. She stepped onto the cable car and turned around to help Philip and Leah.

"Grant!" she yelled, frantically searching the passengers for her brother. "Where's Grant?" she screamed. "STOP this ride!"

"Don't worry, young lady," said the cable car driver. "I'll call back to the ticket taker and make sure he gets on the next car coming up."

Tears ran down Christina's face. As the Skyride pulled away, she saw her little brother's blond head disappear as he ran down the mountain.

21
DOWN THE
RABBIT HOLE

"Whoooa!!" said Grant as he half ran, half slid down the side of Stone Mountain. Icy rain was beginning to pelt down, stinging his face. He pulled his green sock cap out of his jacket pocket. He shoved it down over his ears and pulled his wool scarf up around his mouth. Overhead, he could see the skylift passing by, headed for the base of the mountain. "I'll climb down and find Christina," he said to himself as he ran.

Grant heard a man's voice yell at him. It sounded vaguely familiar, but was it friendly? He could not take a chance. He ran faster. *This IS a big rock*, he thought. His feet slipped and slid as though he wore ice skates.

A thick, white bank of fog crept up the side of the mountain. What appeared to be rock was, in reality, nothing—nothing but empty, white sky. And it was into this nothingness—hundreds of feet in the fog—that Grant stepped.

Like Alice falling through the rabbit hole in *Alice in Wonderland*, Grant fell from whiteness into whiteness. His arms flew straight up over his head as he plunged down, down, down. At first, he could feel the stubble of brush and loose rock against the back of his legs—then nothing. Down...down...THUD!

Somehow, somewhere, Grant had landed.

I can't be at the bottom of the mountain, thought Grant. *I'm still alive*. He wiggled his arms and shook his legs. Carefully, he felt at arm's length all around. He could see nothing but thick fog. Behind him was the steep wall of the mountain. He seemed to have landed on a ledge, a very smooth ledge covered with a slick coating of ice. *How wide is this*, he thought, carefully moving his foot around. He realized that it was flat around his feet, but then it tapered off toward a smooth, rounded edge.

The fall had happened too fast for Grant to be scared. But now, he was terrified. "And I thought the elevator at the Peachtree Plaza was scary," he said aloud.

Suddenly, the ghostly fog began to stir. The thick tufts of cloud that seemed to hold him against the mountainside turned into thin, white shreds moving all around him. They seemed to pull him away. The fog moved wispily up the mountain, and suddenly, Grant saw the ground beneath him—far, far beneath him!

"AAAAAAAAAAA!" Grant let out a long, wailing scream. He had slipped down the steepest side of the mountain—down the side with the carving of the Civil War generals on it.

"I'm perched on the earlobe of General Robert E. Lee!" he yelled.

Then, Grant's worse nightmare happened. He began to slide. The smooth granite ear was now coated in a thick sheet of ice. The bottoms of his sneakers were like glass slippers against the ice. Both feet began to move forward. Grant stooped down, but the shift of his weight propelled him ahead even faster, fractions of an inch at a time, but forward, forward down the ear. There was nothing to grasp, nothing to hold on to! Grant wrapped his arms around himself and closed his eyes.

22
SNOW FALL

Grant snuggled down into his sleeping bag on the couch in the living area of their room at the Peachtree Plaza. Mimi handed him a steaming mug of hot chocolate, piled high with whipped cream and sprinkled with peppermint flakes.

Grant," Mimi said, "I don't know what possessed you to run down that mountain. Why didn't you wait for the next cable car? Please promise me you will never do something that foolish again." She patted his forehead.

"I'm sorry, Mimi," Grant said.

Mimi sighed. "I'm so glad you're not hurt. But you were very lucky. Now, I'm going to type up some notes. Let me know if you need something."

"My ears are still throbbing from the sound of those helicopter rotors," Grant said when Mimi left the room. "But I'm glad you called the park rescue squad, Christina," he added quickly.

"We called them, but they had already sent a chopper," she said. "Someone else must have seen you fall down the mountain."

"That rescue guy grabbed my arm," said Grant, springing from his sleeping bag. "Then he yelled, 'Don't move and close your eyes.' And there I was—dangling hundreds of thousands of feet above the earth!"

Christina rolled her eyes at Grant's exaggeration. "OK, Grant," she said. "You're getting a little carried away!"

"Can I be the rescue guy?" asked Philip, jumping up from the floor. The two boys acted out Grant's rescue, trading parts and embellishing the drama.

"We flew so close to that carving," said Grant, "I could see a tree growing out of Stonewall Jackson's nose!"

"You WERE that carving!" cried Philip. The boys screamed with laughter.

Leah and Christina laughed, too, but Christina felt guilty. If anything had happened to Grant, it would have been her fault.

"What happened to the men?" Grant asked.

"We never saw them again," said Christina. She turned on the television.

"As you can see, snow is falling in Atlanta," said the news reporter. "Forecasters predict there will only be an inch. We do not expect it to delay the lighting of the Great Tree tonight. This is Brianna Brown reporting live from downtown Atlanta."

Christina ran to the picture window. She flung open the drapes.

It was snowing! A white blanket covered all of Atlanta below them. The capitol looked like the top of a wedding cake. All the clean gold hid beneath white icing, just as the gold had once been snug beneath the snow in the Dahlonega gold mines.

"Gosh, there's someone up on the dome in this snow," said Christina. The kids watched as one lone man worked on the snowy dome.

Suddenly, Christina realized something. She shuddered. The bits and pieces that had made no sense to her began to flutter into place like a snowflake puzzle. But what did that piece of paper mean? And why did those men want it so badly?

23

THE PINK PIG

Coats, hats, scarves, mittens, and four happy faces were stuffed into the backseat of Papa's car. Papa pulled into Lenox Square, a huge shopping mall in Atlanta's Buckhead neighborhood. They were headed for the Lighting of the Great Tree, a holiday tradition in Atlanta for decades.

"Wow!" said Grant, spotting the tree on top of the mall's roof. "That's one huge tree!"

Mimi told them how every year a gigantic tree was hoisted to the top of the old Rich's Department Store in downtown Atlanta when she was a young girl. "It was always a magical moment when they lit the tree," she said. "Carolers sang and Santa Claus arrived. The holiday season officially opened."

She said in later years, the tradition was moved to the rooftop of Macy's at Lenox Square. There was more room there for the huge crowds that attended.

"We would also ride the Pink Pig," she added.

Grant's ears perked up. "You rode a pig, Mimi?" he asked incredulously. He giggled at the thought of Mimi, in her red high heels, atop a squirming, snorting pig.

"I did!" said Mimi. "The Pink Pig is a little children's monorail that traveled along the ceiling at Rich's. It would fly over the toy department. We never missed it. Now, it runs on a little train track in a tent here at Lenox."

As Mimi talked, Christina plotted what to do to solve the mystery. Her plan required two things. One was that the men chasing them would show up. The second was that they would get away from Papa and Mimi. She was not certain they could accomplish that. But once inside the crowded mall, Christina realized the Pink Pig was the key.

"Can we go ride the Pink Pig?" she asked Mimi.

"Aren't we too old?" said Leah.

"I'm not too old," said Philip, frowning at his sister. "I've never ridden the Pink Pig."

"Heck, you're never too old to ride Priscilla, the Pink Pig," said Mimi, looking misty-eyed.

"It has a name?" asked Grant. "Pris...what?"

"Priscilla," said Mimi, looking at her watch. "You have time before the tree lighting."

With a wave, Christina dashed away with Grant, Leah, and Philip close behind.

Once out of Mimi and Papa's sight, Christina spun around and gathered the other three around her. "I've got it figured out," she said. "Or at least partly."

"The mystery?" asked Grant.

"Today, I recognized someone on the capitol dome," she said. "One of the men from Stone Mountain."

"So?" Philip said, tugging at Christina's sleeve to encourage her to walk while she talked.

"Do you really want to ride the Pink Pig?" Christina asked Philip.

"Yes!" said Philip and Grant in unison.

"Look, I don't think it's a coincidence that man was up there," continued Christina. "What I think is—"

Grant interrupted her. "What I think is we'd better get out of here!" He motioned behind them.

Walking quickly through the mall were Snatch and the bus-jacker. Even in the mall jammed with holiday shoppers, they had spotted the kids.

"Let's go!" Christina shouted. The kids tore around a jewelry cart vendor. They ducked in and out of groups of shoppers and beneath bulging shopping bags. They scrambled up the first escalator they saw.

Christina spotted the entry sign for the Pink Pig. She never really had any intention of getting on a ride meant for little kids. But now, it seemed the only way out of this mess.

Embarrassed, she quickly purchased four tickets and climbed aboard with Leah and a very eager Grant and Philip.

"Did we lose them?" asked Grant happily.

"No, they're trying to get aboard, but they can't sit in the little piggy cars!" said Christina, who was watching the men. Slowly the Pink Pig pulled away for its ride through Pink Pig Storyland.

"We can't ride this thing all night," said Leah.

"No, we can't," said Christina. "But we have to catch them off guard. The ticket says the Pig goes around twice. When I say 'jump,' just jump off and head away from here."

Philip turned to Grant with a worried look on his face. "No worries," said Grant. "If I jumped off a mountain, we can jump off a pig!"

The Pink Pig slowed as it came around to the end of its first loop. The men were still standing at the entrance. Bravely, Christina looked them in the eye as the Pink Pig passed by them.

But before the Pig could start another circle through Storyland, Christina said, "Jump!" The last thing Christina saw as she looked over her shoulder was the surprised faces of the two men desperately trying to get around shoppers and Pink Pig barricades. Then she swung back around and raced through the mall.

What Christina didn't notice was Mr. Black Trenchcoat intently watching them and talking into his cell phone.

24
LIGHTING UP
THE GREAT TREE

The kids dashed through Lenox Square Mall. They sprinted up escalators and down stairs. They darted past a line of kids waiting anxiously for Santa. They scrambled around huge cardboard ornaments, candy canes, and toy soldiers. People were eating. People were shopping. People were lugging huge shopping bags and pushing strollers filled with babies and more shopping bags.

Carolers in long, red robes stood in the mall's main lobby. Cameras and television crews stood nearby, filming the holiday festivities. The area was filled with vendors displaying decorative mountains of gourmet goodies—chocolates, jams, teas, and coffees. A harried sales clerk was supervising the loading of Coke bottles from a tall pyramid display. He saw Christina staring at him. "Someone just bought the whole thing!" he explained in astonishment.

But then Grant shouted, "They're closing in!"

Christina and Philip broke one way, while Grant and Leah went the other. They knocked over the pyramid of Coke bottles. From the surprise shower of shattered green glass oozed a gooey, yellow mess.

"Yuck!" Grant said, wiping his hands on his pants as they ran. He screwed up his face. "Whoever bought this stuff will be really sorry!"

Within minutes, the men chasing them slipped and slid in the sticky mustard goo. The carolers craned their necks to see what the commotion was. The clerk looked panic stricken.

A weary Christina shouted, "C'mon!" Whatever thoughts she had about solving the mystery were out of her head.

She shoved open a stairwell door at the end of a long, crowded corridor. The kids bolted up the flight of steps. Having no idea where they were or where they were going, the four pushed open a metal door. It slammed heavily behind them.

The kids found themselves on the dark, snow-covered roof. They were face-to-face with the Great Tree, soaring high into the dark, cold night.

Suddenly, the door banged opened behind them and four men lunged out. Christina recognized the men. They were Bus-Jacker, Snatch, The Mask, and Mr. Smooth Voice.

Christina boldly turned to them. "I know what you guys are doing!" she shouted at the men. They took a step back in surprise. "You've been stealing the gold off the capitol dome!"

One of the men laughed. "It's stolen, kid," Mr. Smooth Voice replied.

Christina turned to the kids. "The note they want so bad from us tells how to reconvert the gold," she said. "The note says, 'Au reconversion process' and some numbers. 'Au' is the symbol for gold on the periodic table of the elements! These guys melted the stripped gold. Now, they don't know how to turn it back into gold."

All four men stiffened and looked menacingly at the kids.

"So you do have the note," Snatch said. "You probably had it all along." He started toward Grant but was stopped by an outburst from Christina.

"Yeah!" she said. "You melted it down and put it in Coke bottles. No one would ever think to look for the capitol dome gold in a Coke bottle! And now you're trying to sneak it out of the city, aren't you?"

Then Grant piped up, "Au reconversion process: H_2O...12...millimeters acid ointment ...heat 312 degrees Centigrade—"

"Wait, kid!" ordered Bus-Jacker, pulling a pencil from his pocket.

Grant shouted numbers, degrees, and formulas as fast as he could make them up.

"Got it," said Bus-Jacker when Grant sputtered out the last of the formula. "Now, what do we do with them?"

All at once, amidst a great roar from below, the lights of the Great Tree burst on in the brilliant colors of Christmas. Each beach ball-sized light danced. Cheers wafted up in the icy night air from the cheerful onlookers standing below.

The roof was a blaze of light and activity. Camera crews, set up on the rooftop to record the event, were rolling. Two helicopters hovered overhead taking pictures. Carolers began singing *We Wish You A Merry Christmas*.

And lastly, from behind the Great Tree, stepped Santa Claus with a dozen GBI agents dressed in black behind him!

The bad guys put their hands in the air.

25

JUST IN THE NICK OF TIME!

"You're right, Christina," said Santa, stepping forward. "The gold from the capitol dome is sealed in thousands of Coke bottles all over town. It's anyplace the thieves had an accomplice. And men in high places always have plenty of accomplices."

"It was O'Hare's doing," The Mask swore with **rancor**.

Grant's head jerked up.

"O'Hare?" Christina muttered, knowing the name was familiar.

"Sorry I couldn't rescue you kids sooner," Santa said. "It was only because you were bugged that I found you. But I only put the pieces together myself tonight. And just in the nick of time, I might add," he said with a laugh. "The shipments were scheduled to leave Atlanta tonight."

Christina, Grant, Leah, and Philip all looked at each other in confusion.

"Bugged?" said Grant.

"Rescued?" said Christina.

They didn't understand what Santa was talking about. But it sounded good.

"I put the wire on the underside of your jacket collar when you fell out of the bus," Santa said to Grant. "I sure was glad you wore the same jacket when you landed on Robert E. Lee's ear!"

Grant looked confused. Then Santa took off his red hat, his white beard, and his red coat. Christina gasped. It was Mr. Black Trenchcoat!

Just then, Mimi and Papa pushed through the metal door behind the men, who were being handcuffed by Santa's agents.

"Thank goodness you are safe!" said Mimi. "We were looking all over for you when you didn't answer my text. I was afraid you were going to miss the Lighting of the Great Christmas Tree."

"But you ended up being a part of the production," said Papa. "We looked up and saw you on the monitors all over the mall."

"We were on TV?" Grant asked, his blue eyes bright with excitement.

"Yes, you were, Grant—again!" said Mimi. "But I think you've got some explaining to do." She turned toward Mr. Black Trenchcoat. "And you do too, Santa," she said with a little bit of a smile.

"My apologies," said Santa. "And I promise I will explain more later. Meantime, I think the city jail's going to have some company for the holidays."

Mimi, Papa, and the kids cautiously slid by the angry men and opened the door to the stairway.

Grant took one look back at the scene and shook his head. "I didn't know until now," he said, "that Santa Claus wore a trench coat!"

26
GOOD AS GOLD!

It was Christmas Eve. Mimi, Papa, the kids, and their parents were standing on the steps of the Georgia State Capitol Building.

"A desperate political candidate might do anything to get money for reelection," Mr. Black Trenchcoat explained. Of course, the kids now knew his real name. Instead of Mr. Trenchcoat, he was Ray Jones, Georgia Bureau of Investigation Undercover Agent for Special Affairs.

"Mr. O'Hare was involved in all kinds of shady deals," Agent Jones went on. "Getting the contract to clean the capitol dome was irresistible. He set up a fake company to steal the gold."

"He sure looked desperate the first time we saw him," Christina said. She could still picture the man in the Peachtree Plaza elevator who wore the VOTE O'HARE campaign button.

"Yeah," said Grant. "I just thought he was afraid I'd throw up on his shoes."

"Sometimes people do crazy things when they are in desperate situations," said Mimi.

"Like jump off Stone Mountain," said Grant.

"Like not give a note back to criminals because she wants to solve a mystery," said Christina.

Even Mr. Jones looked at Mimi. "Like use kids as bait," he said, "to get proof to **subvert** a plot and convict a criminal."

Grant looked puzzled. "I just thought of something," he said. "How are you going to convert the gold back? The note is unreadable!"

Christina laughed. "That's the best part of it," she said. "They could have found that answer on the Internet or in any science textbook!"

The governor of Georgia emerged from the building with a big smile on his face. He handed out certificates to the kids and thanked them for helping solve the case.

"I'm sorry this ceremony has to be top secret until after the trial," he said. "But I know I speak for the people of Atlanta when I say thank you for—" He paused as a sudden surprise flurry of snowflakes descended upon the group, even though the sun was shining on the far horizon.

"Thank you for giving us—" The governor stopped once more as the sun hit the undersides of the fine flakes and made them shine. "For giving us a gold Christmas!"

As everyone headed down the steps, Agent Jones asked, "What can I get you kids for Christmas before I have to get back to work?"

The kids all nodded at one another. There was no doubt!

"Well, Mr. Black Trenchcoat," said Grant with a grin, "how about a ride in your mustard Mustang?"

Agent Jones smiled and looked at the parents. "Sounds great to me," said Mimi. The rest nodded in agreement.

Agent Jones jingled his keys. "Tell me where you want to go," he said, heading for the car.

"Down Peachtree!" Christina said emphatically.

Agent Jones looked perplexed. "But which one?" he asked.

"ALL of them!" Christina, Grant, Leah, and Philip shouted in unison. They ran toward his car, jumping and waving their arms wildly in the air.

Agent Jones opened the door. With a deep bow, he escorted them into his yellow Mustang with shiny black leather seats.

Christina settled against the plush bucket seat and watched the glittering snow hit the windshield. She knew this Christmas was going to be good—as good as GOLD!

Well, that was fun!

Wow, glad we solved that mystery!

Where shall we go next?

EVERYWHERE!

The End

Now...go to
www.carolemarshmysteries.com
and...

- Add this book to your personal Adventure Map Tracker!

- Go on a Scavenger Hunt!

- Take a Pop(corn) Quiz!

- Hear from Mimi, Papa, Christina, and Grant!

- Talk to Christina and Grant!

- Join the Fan Club...and MUCH MORE!

GLOSSARY

cacophony: a lot of harsh, unpleasant noise

convex: curved or rounded like the outside of a sphere or circle

entourage: a group of people attending to or following an important person

fiasco: a thing that is a complete failure

heyday: the time of a person's or thing's greatest success or popularity

kiosk: a small, light structure with open sides used to sell merchandise or services

maliciously: done just to be mean

pirouetted: twirled around rapidly, as in ballet

legible: handwriting or print that is clear enough to read

melodrama: a sensational dramatic piece with exaggerated characters and exciting events intended to appeal to the emotions

palpable: able to be touched or felt

rancor: bitterness or resentfulness, especially when long-standing

subvert: undermine the power and authority of (an established system or institution)

Great Places to Visit in Atlanta

Atlanta Botanical Garden
Atlanta Cyclorama & Civil War Museum
Centennial Olympic Park
CNN
Fernbank Museum of Natural History
Fox Theatre
Georgia Aquarium
High Museum of Art
Martin Luther King, Jr., National Historic Site
Mary Mac's Tea Room
Piedmont Park
Stone Mountain
Sun Dial Restaurant, Westin Peachtree Plaza Hotel
The Varsity
Turner Field
Underground Atlanta
World of Coca-Cola
Wren's Nest
Zoo Atlanta

Enjoy this exciting excerpt from:

THE MYSTERY AT Hollywood

1

HOT WINDS AND SHAKY GROUND!

Bump!

Bump! Bump!

"Yikes!" cried Grant from his seat in the *Mystery Girl*. "My lemonade's spilled everywhere!"

"Nice landing, Papa!" said Christina, handing her little brother some paper towels and chuckling. "Too bad I can't say the same for you, Grant!" She closed her book and placed it in her pink, flowery backpack.

"Guess what?" said Grant. "Papa landed right in the middle of a bunch of mountains!" He pressed his sticky hands against the window. "Wow, look at 'em!"

Papa grinned. He expertly taxied the little red and white plane down the runway of the Bob Hope Airport. "We're here!" he announced.

"Papa's an ace pilot," said his wife, Mimi, patting his hand. "And isn't it a beautiful day in sunny California?"

"Yep," Papa replied, winking at Mimi. "The Santa Ana winds have cleared out most of the smog—just for us, I think!"

"What are Santawins?" asked Grant, screwing up his face. "Did Santa win something?"

Papa laughed his big, booming laugh. "Usually winds blow from the west to the east, but Santa Ana winds blow the opposite way," he explained. "They're dry and warm winds. They blow out of the desert states, across Southern California, and out to the Pacific Ocean. They push all the fog and smog out to the ocean. That's one reason it's so clear today."

"Did you say smog?" asked Grant. "What's that?"

"Smog is the dirty-looking haze that hangs over a city," explained Papa. "It's a combination of smoke and fog. That's why it's called 'smog.'"

"Don't the Santa Ana winds cause fires sometimes?" asked Christina. "I remember learning that when we studied weather in science class."

"Yep," said Papa. "In the summer, they can be hot and dangerous. They can stir up fires in these mountains. And the fires spread like lightning because the winds are so strong."

"A lot of people say that when the Santa Ana winds blow, people act a little crazy. Anything can happen," said Mimi in a deep, mysterious tone.

Christina grinned at her lively grandmother who was always looking for a mystery. After all, Mimi was Carole Marsh, the famous writer of children's mystery stories. Papa flew their plane, the Mystery Girl, all over the world so Mimi could research her novels. Many times Christina and Grant traveled along with their grandparents.

"Do you think you'll find a mystery to write while we're here?" asked Christina.

"You never know," said Mimi, smoothing her short blond hair. Her blue eyes twinkled. "But right now, I just want to concentrate on the screenwriting workshop I'm going to."

"Papa, are you going to stay with us while Mimi learns how to write a movie?" asked Grant.

Papa turned his plane toward a small hangar at the airport. "No, I'm going to be right by her side," he replied. "I'll be fetching her coffee and snacks while she concentrates!"

Mimi winked at Papa. She slipped into one of her favorite red sweaters and buttoned it up.

"Grant, you and Christina are going to hang out with Brianna and Jeremy Reyes," she said. "Their mother, Elizabeth, is the manager of the Hollywood Roosevelt. That's where we're staying. They live right at the hotel and they'll show you around Hollywood. It should be very exciting because next week is the Academy Awards ceremony!"

"A Cat or Me Awards?" said Grant. "That's the weirdest thing I've ever heard!"

"Academy Awards," said Christina, slightly annoyed with her little brother. "They are a really big deal!"

"Academy Awards are awards presented to the best movies and actors of the year," said

Mimi. "The award is a gold statuette of a person they call 'Oscar'!"

"Oscar?" repeated Grant. He shrugged his shoulders and shook his head. "An award they call 'Oscar'! That's even weirder!"

"It's not weird here in Hollywood!" replied Mimi. "Anyway, everyone is preparing for all the celebrities to arrive. They are glitzing it up in Hollywood!" Mimi clapped her hands, making her rhinestone bangles jingle on her wrists.

"Mimi loves her movies," said Papa. He pushed back his black cowboy hat and unbuckled his seat belt.

"They'll be rolling out the red carpet for us, won't they Mimi?" cried Christina. She tossed her stick-straight, chestnut-brown hair and struck a movie star pose.

Christina loved movies as much as her grandma. The idea of visiting Hollywood excited her.

"Hurray for Hollywood," sang Mimi, closing up her red handbag and stepping out of the plane. "That screwy, ballyhooey Hollywood!" She threw her arms out wide.

Christina slung her backpack over her shoulder. She followed Mimi out of the plane. "Hooray for Hollywood!" she sang back. "Where you're terrific if you're even good!"

The two locked arms and danced down the *Mystery Girl's* steel stairway.

"We really need to learn all the words to that song," said Mimi. The wind whipped her short blond hair around her face.

Grant followed closely behind the duo. "Oh, man, I got my iPod all sticky!" he said, pouting. He turned on the music device and shoved it into his pocket. "I wish we could go to Disneyland while we're here." He plopped his blue ball cap onto his unruly blond hair and stuck ear buds into his ears.

Christina lifted up one ear bud. In a deep, low voice she said, "You never know what's going to happen. After all, the Santawins are blowing!"

Grant frowned at her as the group walked toward the airport terminal.

"They filmed scenes from *Indiana Jones* at this airport," announced Mimi, "as well as one of my favorite old movies—*Giant*. When I was a girl, I adored one of the actors in it. His name was—oh, my!"

RUMMMMMMMMBLE! Suddenly, the ground started to shake!

"Whoooooa!" yelled Grant. He yanked out his ear buds and grabbed hold of Christina. "What's going on?!"

"It's a little ol' earthquake," responded Papa. "Welcome to California!"

2
TAR STUCK!

"Don't worry, Grant. It was just a tremor," said Papa, driving their red rental car along the crowded California freeway. "Earthquakes happen all the time in California. The folks who live here probably didn't even notice it."

"Exactly what is an earthquake?" asked Grant.

"We studied earthquakes last year at school," said Christina. "My science teacher said an earthquake is what happens when the earth suddenly releases energy. The earth shifts and creates waves of energy that vibrate through the earth's crust. She said vibrations move out from the earthquake's center just like ripples do when you drop a pebble into water."

"Hey, I know what that looks like!" said Grant. "I throw stuff into puddles all the time."

"The closer you are to the center of the earthquake," added Christina, "the more you feel the vibration."

"I read that there are about half a million earthquakes in the world each year," said Papa. "Most of them can't even be felt, and only about 100 do any kind of damage."

"OK, kids," said Mimi, changing the subject. "Papa and I have a surprise for you. We're going to a special place called the 'La Brea Tar Pits'!"

"What did you say?" cried Grant. "Lab pits?"

"La Brea Tar Pits," said Papa slowly. "*Brea* in Spanish means 'tar.'"

"Yuck! Tar pits! We're going to pits filled with tar?" asked Grant, scrunching up his nose.

"Come on!" said Mimi as Papa stopped the car in the parking lot. "You'll be amazed. Let's go see some wooly mammoth fossils!"